THE
NANCY DREW
NOTEBOOKS®

#54

The Stinky Cheese Surprise

CAROLYN KEENE
ILLUSTRATED BY JAN NAIMO JONES

Aladdin Paperbacks
New York   London   Toronto   Sydney   Singapore

First Aladdin Paperbacks edition June 2003

Copyright © 2003 by Simon & Schuster, Inc.

ALADDIN PAPERBACKS
An imprint of Simon & Schuster
Children's Publishing Division
1230 Avenue of the Americas
New York, NY 10020

The text of this book was set in Excelsior.

Printed in the United States of America
10 9 8 7 6 5 4 3 2 1

Library of Congress Control Number 2002111918

ISBN 0-689-85694-6

The Stinky Cheese Surprise

1

Battle of the Burgers

Only three weeks of summer vacation left," George Fayne sighed.

George's cousin Bess Marvin gasped. "Three weeks?" she asked. "That means summer vacation is practically over!"

Nancy Drew smiled at her two best friends as they walked along Main Street. Then she did the math.

"There are seven days in each week," Nancy figured. "So three weeks times seven days in each week equals . . . twenty-one days."

Bess sighed with relief. "Twenty-one days sounds *much* better!" she said.

It was Monday afternoon. Each of the girls

had gotten permission to go to Hamburger Herbie's on Main Street. Herbie served the best burgers in River Heights.

It was cool for August so the girls wore shorts, sneakers, and light jackets over their T-shirts.

Nancy wore butterfly barrettes in her reddish blond hair. Bess had a pink scrunchie wrapped around her long blond ponytail. George's dark curls bounced freely as usual.

"What fun things should we do for the next three weeks?" Nancy asked. "I mean, the next twenty-one days?"

"We can go to the movies," George suggested. "And to the park."

Bess gave Nancy a wink. "And maybe even solve a mystery!" she said.

Nancy loved solving mysteries. She even had a special blue detective notebook where she wrote down all her suspects and clues.

"Maybe," Nancy said. "But right now, all I can think of is a juicy burger and a yummy-licious root beer float!"

The girls stopped in front of Hamburger Herbie's. Nancy reached to open the door. . . .

"Hey, Nancy!" a girl's voice called.

Nancy turned and saw Brenda Carlton. She was dressed in a yellow suit jacket, matching skirt, and white shoes. Running behind her was eight-year-old Bobby Mercado. Bobby was in Mrs. Keller's third-grade class at Carl Sandburg Elementary School. He was holding a video camera.

"I heard Brenda joined the River Heights Junior Reporter Brigade this summer," George whispered. "They have their own TV channel and everything."

Brenda was in the girls' third-grade class. She wrote her own newspaper, *The Carlton News,* on her computer every week. Brenda was good at reporting the news but not always good at being nice.

"Nancy Drew," Brenda said. She shoved a microphone up to Nancy's face. "Is it true that you went to Space Camp? And flew a spaceship all the way to outer space?"

"No!" Nancy cut in. "But Bess, George, and I did just come back from Echo Lake."

"And the lake was invaded by tiny mutant lizards," Brenda added. "Right?"

"Wrong!" Nancy said. "But we did win

3

second prize in a sand castle contest."

Brenda narrowed her eyes. She motioned for Bobby to shut off the camera.

"Why can't you just go along with it?" Brenda asked the girls. "Then I can report an awesome story."

"That would be lying," Bess said.

"But nothing exciting happened in River Heights all summer!" Brenda wailed.

"Why don't you report on Herbie's great hamburgers?" George suggested.

"Herbie's is *history*!" Brenda scoffed. "Ever since Regal Burger opened two weeks ago all the kids go there instead!"

Nancy glanced across the street. Regal Burger looked like a bright yellow castle. Outside it was a miniplayground with a dragon slide and a unicorn carousel. It was filled with kids.

"*We* ate at Regal Burger last week," George said. "And Herbie's still rules."

"You mean *drools*!" Brenda said meanly. "Come on, Bobby. Maybe someone spotted a two-headed alien at the mall."

"Cool!" Bobby said.

Nancy watched Brenda and Bobby walk

away. "I never saw Brenda wearing a suit before," she said.

"Me neither. She's usually wearing snooty-pants!" George joked.

Nancy was about to open the door to Hamburger Herbie's again when someone else from their class ran over. It was Orson Wong.

Nancy blinked. Orson was dressed in a red-and-yellow jumpsuit. He was also wearing a matching cap and curled shoes that were sewn with bells!

"It's not Halloween yet," Bess said. "Why are you dressed up as a clown?"

"I'm *not* a clown!" Orson snapped. "I won a joke-telling contest and now I'm Regal Burger's Jester of the Week!"

Nancy had read about jesters in a book about old castles. A jester's job was to make the king and queen laugh.

"I get to tell jokes to all the customers," Orson bragged. "Like this one: How do you make a rhino float?"

Nancy, Bess, and George shrugged.

"Add soda and ice cream!" Orson guffawed. "Get it? Get it? Get it?"

George rolled her eyes. "I didn't know Regal Burger served *corn,*" she said.

But Nancy thought Orson's joke was funny.

"Why don't you tell some jokes to the kids at Herbie's, too?" Nancy asked Orson.

"Hamburger Herbie's?" Orson gasped. "If Queen Patty saw me in there I'd lose my jester job!"

"Who's Queen Patty?" Bess asked.

"Queen Patty owns Regal Burger," Orson whispered. He glanced over his shoulder. "And here she comes now!"

Nancy noticed a dark-haired woman crossing the street. She wore a red pantsuit and a gold cardboard crown on her head.

"There you are, Orson!" Queen Patty called out. "I need you to stand outside the castle and hand out smoothie samples."

"Yes, ma'am!" Orson said quickly.

"Then I want you to tell jokes to the customers waiting on line," Queen Patty added. "And make sure they're funny."

The bells on Orson's shoes jingled as he followed Queen Patty back across the street.

"She may not be a *real* queen," George whispered, "but she sure acts like one!"

The girls finally entered Hamburger Herbie's. But something wasn't right. The tables and booths were practically *empty*!

Herbie stood behind the counter. He smiled when he saw the girls.

"Don't tell me—let me guess!" Herbie said. "Three burgers and three root beer floats—heavy on the ice cream."

"Yes, please!" Nancy said happily.

"Where is everybody?" George asked. "This place is usually packed with kids."

"The kids are all over at Regal Burger," Herbie sighed. "I even hired a prize-winning chef from Paris to try to compete, but the kids won't even *try* his burgers!"

Nancy glanced through the square window behind the counter. A man wearing a floppy chef's hat was flipping burgers in the kitchen.

"Three burgers coming up!" Herbie said as he turned toward the kitchen.

As the girls headed toward a table Nancy felt sorry for Herbie.

"There must be something Herbie can do

to bring the kids back," Nancy told her friends. "But what?"

"Herbie doesn't have room for a dragon slide," George said. "Or a carousel. Or even—"

"Ohmigosh!" Bess cut in. Her hand trembled as she pointed. "Look!"

Nancy looked toward where Bess was pointing. She saw a tiny green lizard-type creature tottering between the tables. It made a whirring noise as it walked.

"Mutant lizards are invading Herbie's!" Bess cried. "Brenda was right!"

George shook her head and laughed. "That's Windup Wally, Bess," she said. "He's the hottest toy around this summer."

"How did Windup Wally get in here?" Nancy asked, looking around. "He couldn't have walked in all by himself."

Emily Reeves poked her head inside the door. "He's *my* Windup Wally," she giggled. "I wound him up outside and aimed him right through the door!"

Nancy smiled as eight-year-old Emily walked into Herbie's. Nancy hadn't seen her all summer.

"My mom is at the store next door," Emily explained. "She said I could come in and say hi."

Emily picked up her Windup Wally. His legs moved back and forth even as she held him.

"How did you get a Windup Wally, Emily?" George asked. "I heard they were all sold out."

"I have *ten* Windup Wallys at home," Emily explained. "They were supposed to go inside my birthday party goody bags."

Nancy remembered getting an invitation to Emily's birthday party in July. Bess and George each got one too. But they all couldn't go.

"Sorry we missed your party, Emily," Nancy said. "We were on vacation at Echo Lake."

"We entered a sand castle contest," Bess added with a smile. "And won second prize!"

But Emily wasn't smiling. "*Everyone* was on vacation!" she complained. "So my mom had to call off the party."

Nancy, Bess, and George frowned.

"You mean you never had a birthday party?" Nancy asked.

"At all?" Bess asked.

Emily shook her head. "Nope. Now I'm stuck with stickers, feather pens, Windup Wallys, and ten empty goody bags!"

Goody bags? Nancy glanced at Herbie, who was behind the counter. Her eyes lit up.

"Bess, George!" she said. "I just got a major brainstorm!"

2

Surprise Party

The girls sat down together at a table. George, Bess, and Emily huddled close as Nancy shared her idea.

"Herbie can give out goody bags to the kids who buy his burgers," Nancy explained. "Regal Burger doesn't do that."

"Great idea!" George said. "And Herbie can call the goody bags zippy bags."

"Why 'zippy'?" Nancy asked.

"Because when the kids find out about the awesome bags," George explained, "they'll *zip* over to Hamburger Herbie's!"

Nancy gave George two big thumbs-up. But Emily looked totally confused.

"Regal Burger? Herbie?" Emily cried. "Can someone tell me what's going on?"

Nancy told Emily all about Herbie's problem. Then Herbie came over with a tray of burgers, and Nancy told him her idea.

"I like it!" Herbie said. He placed the tray on the table. "But where do I get all those great goody bags?"

"We can use Emily's goody bags!" Bess blurted out.

Nancy nudged Bess. It wasn't nice to offer Emily's bags without her permission.

"I was going to save the goody bags for my next birthday party," Emily sighed. "If I ever have another birthday party."

Nancy felt badly. Maybe there was a way to help Herbie *and* Emily.

"Why don't we have a new birthday party for Emily here?" Nancy asked. "We could have it on the day Herbie gives out the zippy bags!"

Emily's eyes lit up. "A birthday party at last!" She swooned with delight. "Thanks!"

Bess began counting on her fingers. "What if more than ten kids show up?" she asked. "We'll only have ten zippy bags."

"I'll be happy if *five* kids show up tomorrow," Herbie explained. "We can try out the ten zippy bags as a test."

Nancy and her friends offered to stuff the ten zippy bags that afternoon. They would give them out the next day at Emily's new birthday party.

"Don't worry, Herbie," Nancy said. "Tons of kids will be eating here again!"

Nancy was about to bite into her burger when someone shouted, "No! No!"

Glancing up, Nancy saw the French chef walking over. His mustache was twitching and his fists were clenched.

"What's wrong, Philippe?" Herbie asked.

"I heard everything!" Philippe snapped in a French accent. "And I did not come all zee way from Paris to cook for a kiddy restaurant!"

"But kids are our best customers, Philippe," Herbie said. "You'll see!"

Philippe muttered something under his breath. Then he stormed back to the kitchen.

"He sounds mean," Bess whispered.

"Yeah," George said. She nodded to her plate. "But he makes a mean burger!"

****

"Bess!" Nancy said. "Those ribbons are for the bags—not your hair."

"Okay, okay," Bess sighed as she yanked the red ribbon off her ponytail.

It was three o'clock in the afternoon. Nancy, Bess, and George were sitting at the Drews' picnic table. The table was covered with feathered pens, sheets of stickers, and ten Windup Wallys.

Emily had helped carry the toys, silver paper bags, and red ribbons from her house to Nancy's. Then she went back home to call everyone about her brand-new birthday party.

Nancy was about to grab a green feathered pen when her Labrador puppy, Chocolate Chip, scurried into the yard.

"Woof! Woof!" Chip barked.

"Chip always barks at squirrels," Nancy said as she picked up the pen.

"A squirrel?" George asked. "Looks more like a rat to me."

Nancy stared at the small creature under Chip's nose. Instead of a bushy tail it had a long skinny one. It *was* a rat!

Bess shrieked, "I hate rats!"

"Aw, put a sock in it, will you?" a boy's voice growled.

Nancy saw Jason Hutchings, David Berger, and Mike Minelli run into her yard. All three boys were in the girls' class. They were also the class troublemakers.

I should have known, Nancy thought as David scooped up the rat. It was his pet, Skeevy.

"We're taking Skeevy to see the new Moleheads from Mars movie," David said. He pointed to his backpack. "I packed tons of his food so he doesn't eat our popcorn."

David tucked Skeevy inside his jacket. Jason pointed to the picnic table.

"Windup Wallys!" Jason cried. "Neat! Can we have some?"

"Sorry," Nancy said, shaking her head. "These toys are for goody bags."

"Another *girlie* party?" Jason sneered. He looked at his watch, then turned to his friends. "Come on. The three-thirty movie starts in ten minutes!"

The boys raced out of the yard.

"I thought I smelled a rat," George muttered. "*Three* of them!"

Nancy and her friends went back to stuffing the zippy bags. When they tied the last ribbon on the last bag they stood up and stretched.

"Let's go into the house for a snack," Nancy suggested. "The zippy bags will be safe here in the yard."

The girls entered the kitchen. Hannah Gruen greeted the girls with a smile. Hannah had been the Drews' housekeeper since Nancy was only three years old.

"How's the Zippy Bag Brigade coming along?" Hannah asked.

"Super, Hannah!" Nancy said. She smiled at the cheese and crackers on the kitchen table. "And those look super too!"

"I used a Dutch cheese called Gouda," Hannah said. "Did you know there are over a hundred different cheeses in the world?"

"That means over a hundred different cheeseburgers!" Bess declared.

When they were finished eating the girls loaded the zippy bags into their bicycle baskets. Then they got permission to pedal to Hamburger Herbie's.

As they parked their bikes Nancy noticed a sign on Herbie's store window. It read: FREE ZIPPY BAGS ON AUGUST 15ᵀᴴ. WINDUP WALLY INCLUDED!

Carefully, the girls carried the zippy bags into Hamburger Herbie's.

"Herbie is in zee kitchen," Philippe said. "So I vill take zee zippy bags."

Philippe seemed more cheerful than before. He showed the girls where he would hide the bags—in the cabinet beneath the ketchup and mustard counter.

"Herbie will be surprised to see all the kids tomorrow!" Nancy said excitedly.

Philippe snickered and said, "Zat won't be his only surprise!"

Nancy had no idea what Philippe meant. But it didn't really matter.

"We'll help hand out the bags when you open the restaurant at noon tomorrow," Nancy offered.

"Très bon!" Philippe said. "That means 'very good' in French."

Nancy smiled to herself. So far everything

was very good. She couldn't wait until tomorrow!

"What a turnout!" Nancy cried.

It was Tuesday and a few minutes before noon. Eight kids were already lined up outside Hamburger Herbie's.

Emily was handing out birthday hats to the kids on line. Even Brenda and Bobby were there to videotape the event.

"Brenda Carlton here with breaking news!" Brenda said to the camera. "As you see, Hamburger Herbie's is *not* history!"

Orson darted across the street with samples of Regal Burger's tangy tacos.

"Who wants tacos *now*?" a boy on line said. "We want burgers and zippy bags!"

At noon Herbie swung the door wide open. He whisked all the kids inside.

"The zippy bags are under the counter," Herbie whispered to Nancy.

"We know," Nancy whispered back.

But as the girls pulled them out, Nancy noticed something weird. The ribbons on the bags looked pink, not red.

"The lights in here are bright," George

said. "Maybe they just look pink."

When every kid was seated, Nancy, Bess, and George handed out the bags.

"Go ahead, kids!" Herbie called out. "See what's inside!"

Bobby's camera rolled as the kids ripped open the bags and tipped them over. But instead of toys, white chunks shaped like triangles dropped out on the tables!

"What is *that*?" George gasped.

"It looks like some kind of . . . cheese!" Nancy said, confused.

The kids also looked puzzled as they pulled off the plastic wrappers. Then—

"Yuck!"

"Phew!"

"Gross!"

Everyone squeezed their noses. The cheese inside the bags was *stinky* cheese!

"Bess, George!" Nancy cried. "What happened to our zippy bags?"

3

Say Cheese!

You girls put stinky cheese in the zippy bags?" Herbie cried. "Why?"

"And where are my toys?" Emily wailed. "How could you do this, Nancy?"

"I-I didn't!" Nancy stammered. She was just as shocked as everyone else.

Nancy stared at the white V-shaped cheeses wrapped in clear plastic. How *did* they get inside the bags?

Bobby kept the camera rolling as the kids dashed out of Hamburger Herbie's.

"You saw it here first!" Brenda said into the camera. "Hamburger Herbie packs a surprise stinker!"

"Oh!" Emily groaned. She placed her hand on her forehead. "Another birthday party ruined!"

Nancy watched as the kids stampeded out of Hamburger Herbie's.

"I don't know how this happened, Herbie!" Nancy insisted. "We put *toys* inside those bags. Honest!"

"Then where did the stinky cheese come from?" Herbie cried.

Nancy didn't have a clue. But she was sure going to find some!

"It's a mystery, Herbie," Nancy said. "And I'm going to solve it."

"It's too late," Herbie groaned. "When word gets out about this, nobody will want to eat here. I'll have to close Hamburger Herbie's for good."

Herbie sulked behind the counter. Nancy could see Philippe through a crack in the kitchen door. He was peeking out with wide dark eyes.

Philippe said something about a *surprise,* Nancy remembered. Could the stinky cheese be it?

"We have to find out who did this," Nancy

told her friends quietly. "But first we need evidence."

Nancy squeezed her nose with one hand. With the other she picked up a wrapped wedge of cheese and slipped it inside her pocket.

The girls left Herbie's. They went straight to the Drews' house to talk about what to do next.

"I'm calling this case 'The Stinky Cheese Mystery,'" Nancy announced.

Bess and George sat around Nancy on the floor in the den. They watched as she opened her notebook to a clean page.

"I know!" George said. "Maybe the culprit stole the toys, then replaced them with the hunks of stinky cheese."

"Or," Nancy said, "the culprit could have *switched* our bags with new ones."

"Switched?" Bess repeated.

"Remember the ribbons?" Nancy pointed out. "They looked pink, not red."

Nancy wrote both ideas in her notebook. Then she started a suspect list.

"The boys wanted the Windup Wallys,"

Nancy said. "They could have come back to steal the toys while we ate our snacks."

"But the boys said they were going to the movies," George pointed out.

Nancy twirled her pencil between her fingers as she thought. "Unless," she said slowly, "they just *said* they were going to the movies."

"But why would the boys be carrying all that stinky cheese?" Bess asked.

"I don't know," Nancy said. "But I do know that the boys are suspects."

Nancy added Jason, David, and Mike in her notebook under Suspects. "The boys are a very good start," she declared.

"Or as they say in French," Bess giggled, *"très bon!"*

French? Nancy's eyes lit up as she remembered Philippe.

"Philippe said he didn't want to cook for kids," Nancy said. "He also said something about a surprise."

"Maybe Philippe used the stinky cheese to scare the kids away!" Bess gasped.

"Write down his name, Nancy!" George

said, jabbing her finger on the page.

Nancy added Philippe's name to the suspect list. They tried to come up with more suspects but couldn't.

"Let's take a TV break," George suggested. "There's a show on now about chimpanzees who write on computers."

"Cool!" Nancy said. She grabbed the remote. But when she gave it a click, she didn't see chimps on the TV screen. Instead she saw—

"Brenda Carlton!" Nancy cried.

Brenda was on TV holding her microphone. Standing next to her was Queen Patty from Regal Burger!

"Queen Patty?" Brenda asked. "What do you think happened at Hamburger Herbie's?"

"Herbie goofed!" Queen Patty said with a grin. "But mix-ups like his won't happen at Regal Burger. And starting tomorrow we'll be handing out our *own* goody bags!"

"Copycat!" Bess snapped.

"You heard it here first, folks," Brenda went on happily. "This is Brenda Carlton for the Junior Reporter Brigade."

Nancy clicked off the television and frowned. Brenda was having too much fun with Herbie's bad luck!

"Could Queen Patty have messed with the bags?" George asked.

"She couldn't know where the bags were hidden," Nancy said. "But we can ask Herbie if she was inside the store."

"Let's ask him now!" George said.

"I can't," Nancy said. "I promised Hannah I'd go to the supermarket with her this afternoon."

She reached into her pocket and pulled out the wrapped cheese.

"And while I'm there," Nancy said, "I might run a little sniff-test!"

"I'm so interested in cheese all of a sudden, Nancy," Hannah said as she piled hunks of cheese into the shopping cart.

So am I, Nancy thought. *But only the stinky kind!*

"Please watch the cart while I run to the next aisle for soap," Hannah said.

After Hannah left Nancy pulled out the stinky cheese. She took a whiff.

"Pee-yew!" Nancy said. Now if she could just match the smelly cheese she was holding with one of the cheeses in front of her!

She leaned over the cheese display and sniffed the cheeses one by one. Until—

"Whoa!" Nancy's head jerked back as she sniffed a hunk of white cheese. The smell matched that of the stinky cheese! Opening her notebook, Nancy carefully wrote the name of the cheese in big letters: LIMBURGER.

I found the name of the stinky cheese, Nancy thought. *Now if I can just find the culprit!*

"'Limburger' rhymes with 'hamburger,'" Bess said Wednesday morning. "I think there's a clue there, Nancy!"

"Maybe," Nancy said. She and her friends were on their way to Hamburger Herbie's. Nancy carried the stinky cheese and her notebook in a small pink backpack.

"Uh-oh," Bess whispered. "We're about to pass David Berger's house."

"And look," George whispered. "David got a new tree house."

But Nancy wasn't looking at the tree house. She was staring at the boys. They were on the grass playing with three Windup Wallys!

4

Trouble up a Tree

Nancy pulled her friends behind a tree on the sidewalk. They peeked out one by one.

"Three Windup Wallys!" George hissed. "Guilty as charged!"

"I just thought of something else," Bess whispered. "'Limburger' rhymes with 'David Berger'!"

"We don't know whether they're guilty yet," Nancy reminded them. "But if they are, where do you think they hid the other toys? Like the feathered pens and the stickers?"

"In the tree house!" George said. "They probably keep tons of stuff up there."

Nancy saw the tree house jutting out from a tall oak tree. The small house was made of wood and painted red. A sign over the door read KEEP OUT! THIS MEANS YOU!

"How can we search the tree house with them in the yard?" Nancy asked.

"Oh, boys!" a woman's voice called.

The front door of the house swung open and Mrs. Berger stepped outside. "Who wants some ice-cold lemonade?" she asked.

"Thanks, Mom!" David called.

The boys scooped up the Windup Wallys and followed Mrs. Berger into the house.

"Are we lucky or what?" Nancy asked. "Let's search that tree house—fast!"

The girls hurried across the yard to the oak tree. They climbed up a wooden ladder and scurried into the tree house.

"What a mess!" Nancy cried. She looked around and saw three jars of bugs, a huge wad of chewed bubblegum, a pile of Moleheads from Mars comic books, and a dirty sneaker hanging from the ceiling.

"Ew!" Bess cried. "How are we going to find pens and stickers in all this?"

"It's a dirty job," George sighed. "But somebody's got to do it."

The girls searched the tree house for the zippy bag toys. But all they found was more yucky junk.

"Hey!" George said. She pointed to three jackets piled in the corner. There were two denim jackets and one gray hooded sweatshirt. "Those are the same jackets the boys wore on Monday."

"Excellent!" Nancy said. "Let's look through the pockets."

"No way!" Bess cried. "You never know what icky stuff we'll find in there!"

"It can't be any ickier than the rest of the stuff in here," George pointed out.

The girls each took a jacket and reached inside the pockets. After pulling out Moleheads from Mars cards, rubber eyeballs, and packs of gum, they found three movie ticket stubs.

Nancy studied the dates and times on all three tickets. "'August fourteenth, three thirty,'" she read out loud. "And they're all for the Moleheads from Mars movie."

"I guess the boys did make the movie after all," George said.

"Unless they got into the movie late," Nancy said. "*After* they messed with our zippy bags."

"That explains the movie," George said. "But where would they get all that stinky cheese?"

Nancy shrugged. "I don't—"

"Eeeek!" Bess shrieked. "I think I just found Skeevy's cage!"

Nancy whirled around. Bess was pointing under a small table.

"Is Skeevy inside?" Nancy asked.

"No!" Bess said with a shudder. "Just some rat toys. And some lumps of cheese."

"Cheese?" Nancy gasped. She peeked under the table and inside Skeevy's cage. Scattered on the bottom were about six hunks of cheese. Suddenly it clicked.

"Hey!" Nancy said excitedly. "On Monday, David said he had packed tons of food for Skeevy. And Skeevy eats *cheese*!"

"The stinky kind?" Bess asked.

"There's only one way to find out," Nancy

said. She pulled the cage out from under the table and examined a piece of cheese from inside. It was dark yellow with round holes.

"It's not the same cheese," Nancy sighed. "It doesn't even stink."

Nancy pulled her notebook out of her backpack and wrote:

The boys aren't guilty because:
1) They had tickets to the movie.
2) The cheese doesn't match.

"I still don't get it," George said. "The Windup Wallys have been sold out since July. How did the boys get three?"

Nancy heard a rustling noise. It came from outside the tree house.

"Uh-oh," Nancy said. "We'd better climb down before the boys get back."

Gripping her notebook, Nancy hurried to the edge of the tree house. Bess and George followed. When they all looked down they gasped.

"The ladder is gone!" Nancy cried.

Jason, David, and Mike ran out from

under the tree house. They were holding the ladder under their arms and laughing.

"Put it back!" George yelled.

"In your dreams!" Jason yelled back.

"Nancy—do something!" Bess said. She shook Nancy's arm and accidentally knocked the detective notebook right out of her hand!

Nancy tried to catch her notebook. Too late! It fell out of the tree house—and into David's hands!

"Oh, no!" Nancy wailed. "Not my detective notebook!"

5

Cheese Grilled

"Awesome!" Jason cried. He flipped through the pages of the notebook. "Nancy's notebook. Are we lucky or what?"

Nancy's heart sank. Her notebook meant everything to her. She couldn't lose it to anyone—especially the boys!

"Give it back!" Nancy shouted. "That notebook is private!"

"Is not!" Jason shouted back. "Our names are written all over this book. Under the word . . . 'suspect.'"

"That's because you're always doing sneaky things!" Bess snapped. "Like taking the ladder away!"

"Put it back!" George demanded.

"No way!" David said. "You're going to be up there forever!"

"That's what you think!" George muttered. She reached out and grabbed a branch. Then she climbed out of the tree house and down the tree.

"Wow!" Nancy told Bess. "I forgot that George is the tree-climbing champ of River Heights."

"You go, George!" Bess cheered.

George snatched the notebook out of Jason's hand. Then she grabbed the ladder and put it right back where it belonged.

"What were you doing up there?" David demanded as Nancy and Bess climbed down.

"Looking for missing toys," Nancy said. "And where did you get those three Windup Wallys you were playing with?"

The boys looked at each other. Then they smiled sneakily.

"Our lips are zipped!" David said.

The boys shut their mouths tightly. Then they ran their index fingers and thumbs across their lips.

"Zipper lips," Nancy mumbled. "Now they'll never talk."

George leaned over and whispered, "Nancy? Where's the stinky cheese?"

Nancy nodded over her shoulder at the pink backpack. What did George want with the stinky cheese now?

She watched as George pulled out the cheese, unwrapped it, and waved it under the boys' noses.

"Yuck!" Mike shouted.

The boys squeezed their noses as they backed up against the oak tree.

"Get it away!" Jason groaned.

George shoved the cheese under Jason's nose and said, "Not until you tell us where you got those Windup Wallys!"

Nancy giggled. Until she saw something pop out of David's shirt pocket. It was his pet rat, Skeevy. The little rat wiggled his nose as he sniffed at the cheese.

"Skeeeeeevy!" Bess shrieked as she raced out of the yard. The boys laughed as Nancy and George ran after her.

"We got the Windup Wallys at Regal Burger," Jason called after them. "Put that

in your notebook, Detective Drew!"

Nancy and George caught up with Bess two blocks away from the house.

"Sorry!" Bess panted. "But you know how much I hate rats!"

"And I dropped the evidence!" George wailed. "I dropped the hunk of Limburger!"

"It's okay, George," Nancy sighed. "I'll never forget that smell anywhere."

The girls discussed the case as they walked to Main Street.

"How did Regal Burger get Windup Wallys for their goody bags?" Nancy asked.

"Maybe Queen Patty had something to do with it," Bess said. "She could have seen Herbie's sign for the Windup Wallys."

Nancy gave it a thought. Queen Patty could have gone inside Hamburger Herbie's—and switched new bags for the zippy bags.

"Let's ask Herbie if he saw Queen Patty inside his store," Nancy suggested.

The girls hurried to Hamburger Herbie's. Once inside Nancy saw Herbie slumped over the counter.

"I'm ruined!" Herbie moaned. "Next week I'll be selling pretzels!"

"I like pretzels!" Bess said.

Nancy walked up to the counter. "Herbie?" she asked. "Has Queen Patty come into your store this week?"

"Queen Patty?" Herbie cried. He laughed out loud. "If Queen Patty herself came in here I would have noticed."

Herbie's right, Nancy thought. *But if Queen Patty didn't switch the bags, how did she get those Windup Wallys?*

"Can we look for clues, Herbie?" Nancy asked. "We'll try to be quiet."

"Make all the noise you want," Herbie sighed. "There's nobody here to care."

The girls searched the cabinet underneath the ketchup and mustard counter. It was dark inside, so they carefully felt around.

"Nothing," Nancy declared.

"There's room between the counter and the wall," George pointed out. "Let's look for clues back there."

The girls squeezed behind the counter.

"Ouch!" Bess cried. "I just stepped on something hard. Like a pebble."

Bess stepped aside. The tiny round object jingled as Nancy picked it up.

"It's a bell," Nancy observed.

The girls shimmied out from behind the counter. Nancy carefully held the bell between her thumb and index finger.

Where did this *come from?* Nancy wondered. Suddenly it clicked.

"Orson's jester costume had bells on the cap," Nancy said. "Maybe Queen Patty sent *Orson* here to switch the bags!"

"No wonder Herbie never saw Queen Patty around here!" George said.

"What do we do now?" Bess asked.

"We have to compare this bell to the ones on Orson's costume," Nancy answered.

Herbie was busy talking on the phone. So the girls left without saying good-bye.

"Now let's find Orson," Nancy said. She began flipping the bell in her palm when—

"Hey!" Nancy cried. She stared at her empty palm. Someone had snatched the silver bell right out of her hand!

Nancy turned and saw Orson racing up Main Street. The bells on his cap were jingling and his fist was tightly clenched.

"He's got our clue!" Nancy shouted. "Stop him! Stop that jester!"

6

Pester Jester

For someone with curly shoes," Bess panted as she ran, "he sure runs fast!"

Nancy, Bess, and George chased Orson down Main Street. Orson skidded around the corner. The girls turned the corner too.

"He's got to be guilty!" George cried. "Why else would he steal our clue?"

Orson picked up speed. But not for long. "Whoa!" he cried as he tumbled down to the sidewalk.

Nancy slowed down. Orson's big curly shoe had gotten stuck in a grate.

"Phooey!" Orson cried. He tried to grab the silver bell as it rolled away.

George picked up the bell and said, "The joke's on you, jester!"

Orson muttered as he freed his foot, "Dumb shoes! Why can't I wear sneakers?"

The girls quickly compared the bell to the one on Orson's cap.

"A perfect match!" Nancy declared.

"Don't tell Patty I was at Hamburger Herbie's!" Orson begged. "Okay?"

"But she sent you there to switch the zippy bags, didn't she?" Nancy asked.

"Switch the bags?" Orson cried. "What are you talking about?"

Nancy told Orson all about the zippy bags and the bell clue. The bells on Orson's cap jangled as he shook his head.

"I didn't steal anything!" Orson insisted. "I just went to Herbie's for a burger, fries, and a shake."

"We thought you only ate at Regal Burger," Bess said.

Orson scrunched up his nose. "Regal Burger's food is *ick!*" he cried. "Herbie's burgers rule big time!"

Nancy couldn't believe her ears. Regal

Burger's Jester of the Week preferred Hamburger Herbie's!

"Didn't you say you'd lose your job if you ate at Herbie's?" Nancy asked.

"I hid behind the ketchup and mustard counter so Patty wouldn't see me," Orson said. "I was so quiet that Herbie didn't even know I was there!"

Nancy wasn't sure if Orson was telling the truth. But she knew a way to find out.

"What flavor shake were you drinking?" Nancy asked. "And what did you put on your burger? Ketchup or mustard?"

Orson shrugged as he tried to remember. "The shake was strawberry. And I always put mayonnaise on my burger."

"Mayonnaise?" George gagged.

"You won't tell Queen Patty I was at Herbie's?" Orson asked Nancy. "Will you?"

Nancy shook her head. "We don't blame you for liking Herbie's burgers better."

Orson sighed with relief. "Thanks," he said. "I owe you one!"

"Then tell us where Patty got Windup Wallys for her goody bags," Bess said.

"She ordered them from the toy maker," Orson said. "Hundreds of them!"

The girls exchanged excited glances. So that's where they came from!

"Good luck with your case," Orson said. He held out his hand for Nancy to shake.

Nancy raised an eyebrow. It wasn't like Orson to wish her luck. But when she grabbed his hand . . .

"Yow!" Nancy cried.

"It's a hand buzzer!" Orson laughed. He showed the plastic gizmo strapped to his palm. "I'm still a jester—so the joke is still on you! Ha, ha, ha!"

"Pest!" George muttered as Orson skipped away.

"Why did you ask Orson those questions about his shake, Nancy?" Bess asked. "And about his burger?"

"Because I want to look for more clues," Nancy answered. "*Messy* ones!"

The girls returned to Hamburger Herbie's. Quickly Nancy searched behind the ketchup and mustard counter. This time she found a bright pink glob on the side of the counter.

"Aha!" Nancy said. "Orson was drinking a strawberry shake. Which proves one thing."

"That he's a slob?" George asked.

"That he was telling the *truth*," Nancy said. She crossed Orson's name out of her notebook. Now the only suspect was the French chef—Philippe.

"Philippe put the bags in this cabinet," Nancy whispered. "And he would have had plenty of time to switch them."

"And as a chef," Bess added, "he would have plenty of cheese."

"Maybe he stashed the *real* zippy bags somewhere in the kitchen," George said.

Nancy turned toward the kitchen. She could see Philippe staring at her from behind the kitchen window.

"We'd better come back tomorrow," Nancy said. "I think something's cooking in the kitchen. And I don't mean burgers!"

"It had to be Philippe, Daddy!" Nancy said during dinner that night. "Who else could have switched the zippy bags?"

Carson Drew smiled as he poured dressing on his salad. "Many cases turn out to be mix-ups, Pudding Pie," he said. "Maybe the cheese got there by accident."

Nancy gave it a thought. Her father was a lawyer and usually had good ideas. But this time Nancy wasn't sure.

"I think somebody did it on purpose, Daddy," Nancy said. "I really do."

Hannah carried a bowl of macaroni and cheese into the dining room. "Surprise!" she exclaimed. "I used extra-sharp cheddar cheese this time."

Nancy gulped at the bright yellow cheese bubbling over the hot macaroni. She usually loved macaroni and cheese. But not this time.

"Thanks, Hannah," Nancy sighed. "But I don't think I can eat any more cheese. Not until this case is over!"

"Way to go, Herbie!" Nancy said at Hamburger Herbie's the next day. "You have a customer!"

The girls looked at the man sitting in the corner booth. A napkin was stuffed into his collar as he bit into a burger.

"Not just *any* customer," Herbie whispered.

"That's Cyril Larder. He's the food critic of *Today's Times*."

"What's a food critic?" Bess asked.

"He writes about restaurants in River Heights," Herbie explained. "He is doing an article on restaurants that have been in River Heights for years. And he's going to write about Hamburger Herbie's!"

"Cool!" Nancy exclaimed. "He'll write good things for sure!"

"I'm keeping my fingers crossed," Herbie joked. "And my toes, too!"

Herbie began polishing napkin holders. Nancy could see Philippe through the kitchen window. He was busy shaking a basket of fries over a vat of oil.

"How do we keep Philippe busy while we search the kitchen?" Nancy whispered.

"Watch this!" George said. She knocked on the kitchen door and Philippe opened it.

George whispered something in Philippe's ear. Philippe flashed a huge smile. He straightened his apron and hurried over to Cyril Larder's table.

"What did you say, George?" Nancy wanted to know.

"I told him Cyril was writing about his cooking," George said. "And that he probably had a ton of questions for him."

"Good work!" Nancy said as they slipped into the kitchen.

The girls searched under counters and inside cabinets. Just when Nancy thought they had checked everywhere, she saw a tall cupboard standing in the corner.

"Let's look inside there," Nancy suggested. She pulled the handle on the cupboard door. It wouldn't open.

She gritted her teeth and yanked it hard. Finally the door swung open.

"Ohmigosh!" Nancy gasped as she spotted a shelf filled with silver bags.

"Nancy, look out!" George cried.

She pulled Nancy back just in time. The girls shrieked as a bucket of eggs fell from the top of the cupboard to the floor with a huge crash!

7

Cook or Crook?

At least we found the zippy bags," Bess said with a shudder.

Nancy stared at the silver bags inside the cupboard. Each one had a red ribbon tied around it. Just like the missing zippy bags!

Next she stared at the broken eggshells and gooey yolks on the kitchen floor. "Look!" she said. "There's a string attached to the bucket handle. The other end of the string is attached to the cupboard door."

"It was a trap!" George said. "Philippe must have set a trap to keep us away from the zippy bags!"

"What is the meaning of zees?" an angry voice demanded.

Nancy spun around. Standing at the kitchen door was an angry Philippe!

"So!" Philippe snapped. "I see you found zee zippy bags!"

"Why did you set a trap?" Nancy asked Philippe. "To protect the zippy bags that you *stole*?"

Philippe's chef's hat flopped back and forth as he shook his head. "It was to protect my secret recipes!" he said.

"Secret recipes?" Nancy repeated.

Philippe stepped over the eggshells to the cupboard. He reached behind the zippy bags and pulled out a metal box.

"*Voilà!*" Philippe exclaimed. He ran his hand over the box. "You'd be surprised how many people want my recipe for Duck L'Orange!"

George shook her head as if she didn't believe Philippe. "Who cares about orange ducks?" she said. "Did you replace the real zippy bags with the stinky cheese bags?"

"Why would I do something like zat?" Philippe scoffed.

"You said you didn't want to cook for kids," Nancy pointed out. "You also said there would be some big surprise."

The word "surprise" made Philippe's shoulders drop. "I did plan a surprise," he sighed. "A big surprise!"

"Then what was it?" Nancy asked.

"Look inside zee zippy bags!" Philippe urged. "And see for yourselves!"

Nancy, Bess, and George each grabbed a zippy bag. They opened them and smiled.

"There's Windup Wally!" George exclaimed. "And the stickers!"

"And a feathered pen!" Bess said.

"And a chocolate lollipop?" Nancy asked, confused. "I don't remember putting lollipops in the zippy bags!"

"I decided zat having kids here would be *très bon!*" Philippe explained. "So I secretly whipped up my special chocolate lollipops to put in zee bags."

Nancy studied her lollipop. It was shaped like the Eiffel Tower in France.

"When Herbie was busy, I sneaked zee zippy bags into zee kitchen," Philippe went on. "Then I threw in zee chocolate lollipops."

"Then what happened?" Nancy asked.

"I was about to return zee bags," Philippe said. "But then I saw a messenger delivering *more* bags to Herbie."

"More?" Bess asked. She pointed into the cupboard. "We only brought these ten!"

"Unless those were the bags with the stinky cheese!" Nancy said excitedly.

"I kept zee zippy bags in zee kitchen," Philippe went on. "I was going to bring them out in the morning when zee birthday party began."

"Why didn't you?" George asked.

"It was too late," Philippe sighed. "Zee kids had found zee cheese in the other bags. And they were running out."

"Why didn't you tell Herbie you had the real bags?" Nancy asked.

"I felt like it was my fault!" Philippe wailed. "I should never have sneaked zee real bags into zee kitchen!"

"Don't feel bad, Philippe," Nancy said. "You did a really good thing!"

"Yeah!" George said. She unwrapped a lollipop and gave it a lick. "And these chocolate lollipops rock!"

"Merci!" Philippe said. He gave a shrug. "It beats flipping zee burgers."

Nancy placed her bag back in the cupboard. "Let's keep the zippy bags here in case the kids come back," she suggested. "And they *will* come back!"

The girls left the kitchen.

"So someone delivered the stinky cheese bags here," George said. "But who?"

Nancy walked over to Herbie and asked, "Do you remember who delivered the zippy bags here on Monday?"

"Hmm," Herbie said. He stroked his chin thoughtfully. "I think it was a delivery service called Twinkle Toes."

"Twinkle Toes," Nancy repeated. She wrote the name in her notebook. "Thanks!"

On the way out the girls passed Cyril Larder. He had three empty hamburger wrappers and two empty cups on his tray. He was smiling as he wrote in his pad.

"Let's go to my house and call Twinkle Toes," Nancy said.

"Why?" Bess asked.

"Someone hired Twinkle Toes to deliver the stinky cheese bags," Nancy explained.

"Maybe they can tell us who."

Once home the girls found Twinkle Toes Delivery Service in the fat yellow phone book. Nancy quickly made the call.

"Twinkle Toes," a woman's voice answered. "We're fleet on our feet!"

"Hello," Nancy said. "Can you please tell me who sent ten zippy—I mean goody—bags to Hamburger Herbie's on Monday?"

"Sorry," the woman answered. "That's private information."

"Please?" Nancy asked.

George grabbed the receiver from Nancy. "Can you at least tell us if the bags smelled like stinky cheese?" she asked the woman.

Click!

"She hung up!" George complained.

Nancy, Bess, and George plopped down on the sofa.

"Now what do we do?" Nancy groaned.

"Oh, girls!" Hannah said as she entered the den. "I've got great news!"

Nancy smiled at Hannah. She could use some good news for a change!

"I've decided I like cheese so much," Hannah went on, "I joined a special club."

"What club?" Nancy asked.

"The River Heights Cheese Lovers Club," Hannah replied. "Every month they meet to taste a new cheese."

"Really?" Nancy asked. "What cheese are they tasting this month?"

Hannah wiped her hands on her apron. "I already missed this month's meeting," she said. "But I think it was Limburger."

Nancy sat up straight. Then she jumped off the sofa.

"Limburger?" Nancy gasped. "That's our stinky cheese!"

8

Herbie Rules!

Nancy!" Bess exclaimed. "Do you think the cheese club knows something about the bags?"

Nancy nodded. "What else but a cheese club would use bags of cheese?" she asked.

Hannah tilted her head. "Does this have something to do with your mystery, Nancy?" she asked.

"Everything!" Nancy replied.

"Then I hope this helps," Hannah said. She showed Nancy a flyer from the cheese club. "The club is run by a couple named Jack and Jill Monterey. They also own a cheese shop on Juniper Street called Say Cheese."

Nancy studied the flyer. "We have to question the Montereys," she said. "I have a funny feeling they know something."

Hannah drove Nancy, Bess, and George to the Say Cheese shop. She waited in the parked car while the girls went inside.

"Say cheese!" a woman announced. She held up a camera and snapped a picture of the girls.

Nancy blinked from the flash. "Are you Mrs. Monterey?" she asked.

The woman smiled. She had short dark hair and wore a clean yellow smock.

"Call me Jill," she said cheerily. She nodded at a bulletin board on the wall. It was covered with photos of smiling people. "And now you can be in our gallery of cheese-lovers too!"

Nancy glanced around the shop. She saw shelves and counters filled with all different kinds of cheeses. There were even sculptures and statues made out of cheese.

"Look!" Bess exclaimed. "There's a cat statue made out of cheese!"

"That's something you don't see every day," George said.

"All of the sculptures were created by my husband, Jack," Jill said.

She pulled aside a white curtain. Behind it sat a man carving a huge hunk of yellow cheese. He had sandy brown hair and was wearing a blue apron.

"Here he is," Jill announced. "Jack Monterey—the family artist."

"A regular Vincent van Gouda," Jack joked. He winked. "A little cheese humor."

Nancy giggled. Then she asked the couple about their cheese club.

"The last meeting was bad news," Jack sighed. "We all went to a restaurant to celebrate the wonders of Limburger. But the cheeses were never delivered."

Nancy's heart began to pound. Were the cheeses delivered to Herbie's instead?

"Can you please tell us the name of the restaurant you went to?" Nancy asked.

"It was a seafood restaurant," Jill replied, "called Halibut Herb's."

"Halibut Herb's!" Nancy repeated. The name sounded like Hamburger Herbie's!

"The delivery service insisted they brought it to the right place," Jack said.

He shook his head. "But I don't think so."

"Was the name of the delivery service Twinkle Toes?" George asked.

"How did you know?" Jill asked.

Nancy shivered with excitement. The pieces were finally falling into place. But she still had a few questions.

"What kind of bags were the cheeses packed in?" Nancy asked.

Jill looked surprised by Nancy's question. But she answered anyway. "They were in silver bags," she said. "With pretty pink ribbons."

"Silver bags!" George cried.

"Pink ribbons!" Bess gasped.

"The stinky cheese bags!" Nancy exclaimed. "Yes!"

"Excuse me?" Jill asked.

Nancy told the Montereys all about the mix-up.

"So that's where our bags went!" Jack said. He shook his head and smiled. "It sure was a mystery to me!"

"And to us!" Nancy giggled. She looked at Bess and George from the corner of her eye. They were giggling too!

"You know," Jill said, "this Hamburger Herbie's sounds like a great place to have our next meeting."

"Herbie would *love* that!" Bess said.

The girls were all smiles as they left the shop and headed toward Hannah's car.

"So that's how the stinky cheese bags landed up at Herbie's!" George said. "They went to the wrong restaurant."

"It *was* a mix-up!" Nancy declared.

"Let's tell Herbie right away," Bess said. "He'll be so happy to find out."

"No, he won't," George sighed. "Even if it was a mistake, what kid would go back to Hamburger Herbie's now?"

As Hannah drove the girls to Main Street, Nancy frowned. George was right. They solved the mystery. But they didn't really solve Herbie's problem.

But when they walked inside Hamburger Herbie's, Nancy's jaw dropped. The place was packed with kids and grown-ups eating burgers. Even Brenda and Bobby were there with their news camera.

"You heard it here first, folks," Brenda was saying. "Cyril Larder of *Today's Times* has declared in the evening edition that Herbie's burgers are the *best* in town!"

"Wow!" Nancy said. "The food critic *did* write good things about Herbie's!"

Herbie was busily handing out trays filled with burgers and floats. Emily was there too, handing out the real zippy bags—with the red ribbons.

"Everyone is here! I'm going to pretend this is a real birthday party at last!" Emily called to Nancy.

Nancy looked around. Everybody *was* there. Even Jason, David, and Mike!

"I hope you didn't bring Skeevy!" Bess said with a shudder.

"Skeevy wouldn't fit in my pocket today," David explained. He laughed as he reached into his pocket and pulled out a wiggly rubber spider. "But this did!"

"Ew!" the girls cried.

As the boys raced each other to a table, Nancy saw Orson Wong. He was sitting at a table and eating a cheeseburger. But this time he wasn't hiding.

"What are you doing here, Orson?" Nancy asked. "Won't you lose your jester job

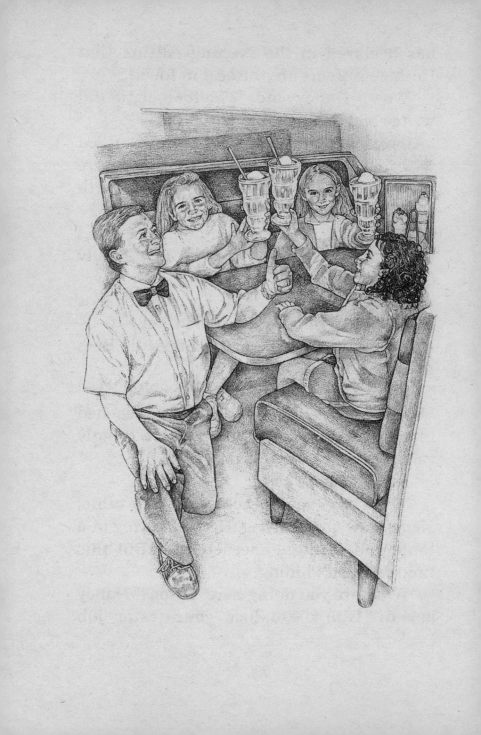

if Queen Patty sees you eating here?"

Orson's cap of bells jingled as he tossed it aside. "I already *quit*," he said. "I'd rather eat like a king than act like a fool anyway!"

The girls decided to celebrate with some root beer floats.

"You did it, Nancy!" Bess said as they all sat down. "You cracked the stinky cheese case!"

"And you saved Hamburger Herbie's from becoming history!" George added.

Nancy shook her head. "Cyril Larder saved Hamburger Herbie's," she said. "And if the kids keep coming back, Herbie will be here forever and ever!"

Herbie walked over. When Nancy told him about the zippy bag mix-up he grinned.

"You really *are* a good detective, Nancy Drew!" Herbie said. "Now how about some juicy burgers and frosty floats?"

"Yes, please!" Nancy said happily.

Bess and George talked to Emily while they waited for their food. But Nancy still had work to do. She pulled her pencil and notebook from her pink backpack. Then she began to write.

Daddy was right again! Accidents can happen and so do mix-ups. And I think I learned something else. People are like the ice cream in a root beer float. If they're good they'll always float to the top. Just like Herbie!

Case closed!

THIRD-GRADE DETECTIVES

Everyone in the third grade loves the new teacher, Mr. Merlin.
Mr. Merlin used to be a spy, and he knows all about secret codes and the strange and gross ways the police solve mysteries.

YOU CAN HELP DECODE THE CLUES AND SOLVE THE MYSTERY IN THESE OTHER STORIES ABOUT THE THIRD-GRADE DETECTIVES:

#1 The Clue of the Left-handed Envelope

#2 The Puzzle of the Pretty Pink Handkerchief

#3 The Mystery of the Hairy Tomatoes

#4 The Cobweb Confession

#5 The Riddle of the Stolen Sand

Coming Soon: #6 The Secret of the Green Skin

ALADDIN PAPERBACKS • Simon & Schuster Children's Publishing • www.SimonSaysKids.com

Ready-for-Chapters